Daniel Plays Ball

adapted by Maggie Testa

based on the screenplay "Daniel Plays Ball"

written by Eva Steele-Saccio

poses and layouts by Jason Fruchter

Ready-to-Read

Simon Spotlight

New York   London   Toronto   Sydney   New Delhi

Whoever throws the ball,
picks an animal.

Then we all make its sound.

Miss Elaina picks a dog.

We all say . . .

Miss Elaina throws the ball to Prince Wednesday.

Grr. I missed the ball.

"Keep trying. You will get better," says Prince Tuesday.

"Quack, quack, quack!"

Prince Tuesday throws the ball to Miss Elaina.

She catches the ball.

Miss Elaina throws
the ball to me.

Grr. I miss it again!

"Keep trying. You will get better," says Prince Tuesday.

Miss Elaina throws the ball to me again.

Then I hug the ball.

"Nice catch,"

says Prince Tuesday.

Daniel Plays at School

adapted by Daphne Pendergrass
based on the screenplay "Problem Solver Daniel"
written by Becky Friedman
poses and layouts by Jason Fruchter

Ready-to-Read

Simon Spotlight
New York London Toronto Sydney New Delhi

"What should we do?"

We ask Teacher Harriet.

We talk about
our problem.
We have an idea!

Daniel Gets Scared

adapted by Maggie Testa
based on the screenplay "A Stormy Day"
written by Wendy Harris
poses and layouts by Jason Fruchter

Ready-to-Read

Simon Spotlight
New York   London   Toronto   Sydney   New Delhi

O the Owl is here to play.

"Time to go inside," calls Mom.

"There is something I do when I am scared," says Mom.

I close my eyes and think about playing with Tigey.

Playing with Tigey
makes me happy.
I feel less scared now.

O the Owl closes his eyes.
He thinks about books.

Books make him happy.
He feels a little
less scared now.

Boom!

We hear more thunder.

It scares us again.

"What did your mom say to do when you're scared?" asked O the Owl.

"When you are scared, close your eyes and think of something happy," I said.

And I am thinking about playing with Tigey.

We feel less scared now.

Daniel Feels Left Out

adapted by Maggie Testa

based on the screenplay written by Becky Friedman

and Angela C. Santomero

poses and layouts by Jason Fruchter

Ready-to-Read

Simon Spotlight

New York   London   Toronto   Sydney   New Delhi

My dad and I are on our way home for dinner.

Katerina and O
are playing outside.

My dad sees me frown.

It helps to talk about your feelings!

It is okay to feel sad sometimes.